The Pie Thief

a play by Joy Cowley

Grandma Goodycook

Cousin Sally

Cousin Jack

Sloppy Dog

Grandma Goodycook:
 Apple tree,
 apple tree,
 throw me down
 some apples.
 That's enough.
 Now I can make a pie.
 Beat, beat, beat and cook.
 Mmmm. It does smell good.
 (She goes to the window.)
 Are you all outside?

Others:
 Yes, Grandma Goodycook.

Grandma Goodycook:

I'm going for a walk.
You're not to come in.

Others:

We won't, Grandma Goodycook.

Grandma Goodycook:

Walk, walk, walk.
I'm as hungry as a lion.
Walk, walk, walk.
I'm as hungry as two lions.
(She comes back.) What's this?
Jumping jimminy! My pie has gone.
Cousin Jack! Cousin Jack!

Cousin Jack:
What's the matter,
Grandma Goodycook?

Grandma Goodycook:
My pie has gone.
That's what the matter is.

Cousin Jack:
Don't ask *me* where it is.
I haven't seen it.

Grandma Goodycook:
What about you, Cousin Sally?

Cousin Sally:
Why, Grandma Goodycook, I haven't
so much as sniffed your pie.

Grandma Goodycook:
Did you eat it, Sloppy Dog?

Sloppy Dog:
Wuff, wuff, of course not.

Grandma Goodycook:
One of you is telling a lie.

Others:
Not me, Grandma Goodycook.

Grandma Goodycook:
Oh well, I'll just have
to begin again.
All outside. Go on.

Others:
Yes, Grandma Goodycook.

5

Grandma Goodycook:

Cherry tree, cherry tree,
throw me down some cherries.
That's enough.
Now I can make a pie.
Beat, beat, beat and cook.
Mmmm. It does smell good.
(She goes to the window.)
Are you all outside?

Others:

Yes, Grandma Goodycook.

Grandma Goodycook:

I'm going for a walk.

You're not to come in.

Others:

We won't, Grandma Goodycook.

Grandma Goodycook:

Walk, walk, walk.

I'm as hungry as a tiger.

Walk, walk, walk.

I'm as hungry as two tigers.

(She comes back.)

What's this? Jumping jimminy!

Now my *other* pie has gone.

Cousin Jack! Cousin Jack!

Cousin Jack:
Did you call me,
Grandma Goodycook?

Grandma Goodycook:
You bet your life I did.
I made another pie,
but the greedy thief
has gobbled that, too.

Cousin Jack:
Well don't look at *me*,
because I didn't take it.

Grandma Goodycook:
   Did you eat it, Cousin Sally?

Cousin Sally:
   Why, Grandma Goodycook,
   how could you *ask* such a thing?

Grandma Goodycook:
   Sloppy Dog, was it you?

Sloppy Dog:
   Wuff, wuff. No, not a lick.

Grandma Goodycook:

One of you is telling a lie.

Others:

Not me, Grandma Goodycook.

Grandma Goodycook:

Oh well, I'll just have
to begin again.
All outside. Go on.

Others:

Yes, Grandma Goodycook.

Grandma Goodycook:

Giggle tree, giggle tree,
throw me down some berries.
That's enough.

Now I can make a pie.
Beat, beat, beat and cook.
Mmmmm.
It does smell good.
I'll soon know
who the pie thief is.
(She goes to the window.)
Are you all outside?

Others:
Yes, Grandma Goodycook.

Grandma Goodycook:
I'm going for a walk.
You're not to come in.

Others:
We won't, Grandma Goodycook.

Grandma Goodycook:
Walk, walk, walk.
I'm as clever as a fox.
Walk, walk, walk.
I'm as clever as two foxes.
(She comes back.)
What's this?
Jumping jimminy, no pie!
Cousin Jack!   Cousin Jack!

Cousin Jack:
What do you want,
Grandma ha-ha-ha Goodycook?

Grandma Goodycook:
So it was *you*, Cousin Jack.

Cousin Jack:

Ha-ha-ha.

No, it wasn't.

Ha-ha-ha.

I never ha-ha did.

It was ha-ha-ha

Cousin Sally.

Cousin Sally:

Hee-hee-hee. Why, Cousin Jack,
that's a big hee-hee lie.

It was hee-hee you and Sloppy Dog.

Hee-hee-hee.

Sloppy Dog:

Ho-ho-ho. I never got one bite.

It was ho-ho-ho those two no-goods.

I tried to ho-ho stop them.

Grandma Goodycook:

Well, what do you know?
All three of you have the
giggles from giggle berries.
What shall I do? Let me see.
I don't have any more apples or cherries.

Others:

Oh, what a pity! Ha-ha-ha.
Hee-hee-hee. Ho-ho-ho.

Grandma Goodycook:

And I don't have any more giggle berries.

Others:

Oh, what a pity. Ha-ha-ha.
Hee-hee-hee. Ho-ho-ho.

Grandma Goodycook:
But I *do* have a lot of dishes.

Cousin Jack:
No, Grandma Goodycook!
Ha-ha-ha. No! Not *dishes*.

Grandma Goodycook:
Yes, Cousin Jack, dishes.
And you can wash.

Cousin Sally:
Dishes! Hee-hee-hee.
I'm getting out of here.

Grandma Goodycook:
No, you're not, Cousin Sally.
You can dry.

Sloppy Dog:

Dishes! I hate dishes.
I'm going to hide.

Grandma Goodycook:

Back you come, Sloppy Dog.
You can put them away.

Sloppy Dog:

All right,
Grandma Goodycook.

Grandma Goodycook:

I'm as hungry as
a crocodile.
I'm as hungry as
two crocodiles.
I'll have a big
bowl of soup.